NATA

BY HELEN V. GRIFFITH

ILLUSTRATED BY NANCY TAFURI

GREENWILLOW BOOKS · NEW YORK

Library of Congress Cataloging in Publication Data
Griffith, Helen V. Nata.
Summary: Nata, the fairy, acts oddly on the first day of summer
and the other small insects and animals soon discover the reason.
1. Children's stories, English. [1. Fairies—Fiction.
2. Animals—Fiction] I. Tafuri, Nancy, ill. II. Title.
PZ7.G8823Nat 1985   [E]   85-727
ISBN 0-688-04976-1   ISBN 0-688-04977-X (lib. bdg.)

For
Clare
&
Sarah
H.V.G.

For

Tara

N.T.

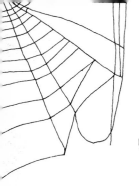

Nata was usually good, but one June day she wasn't.
She tangled the spider's web, spoiling the design.
She climbed the flower stems and shook out all the bees.
She pulled the garter snake's tail.
"Ignore her," advised the toad.
"That's easy to say," said the spider. "It's not your web."
"And it's not your tail," sniffed the snake.

"What's wrong with Nata, anyway?" asked the bees.

"First day of summer," said the toad. "That's what's wrong with Nata."

"No, it's not," said Nata.

She sneaked up on a sleeping cricket and tied its feelers in a knot.

The deer mouse and her babies were watching from their doorway.

Nata made a face at them.

"She usually plays games with us," said a baby mouse.

"And calls us darlings," said another baby.

"She will tomorrow," said the toad.

"No, I won't," said Nata.

Nata picked up a pebble and threw it into the pond.
The fish all darted under lily pads.
Just then the toad called out, "Nata! The cat!"
Nata whirled around. "Scat!" she said.
The cat took a slow step forward. Nata stepped backward.
"Fly, Nata!" squeaked the mice.

"Fly, Nata!" hissed the snake.
"Why doesn't she fly?" buzzed the bees.
  The cat crept forward. Nata stepped backward.

"I can't look," said the spider.

The cat leaped. Nata jumped back.
She slipped into the pond with a tiny splash.
The cat scooped Nata up with his paw, spinning her
out of the pond and across the grass.
The toad plopped on top of her and
glared at the cat. "Brute," she said.
The cat tried to look under the toad.
"I dare you," said the toad, puffing herself up.
The cat paused. Then he stalked out
of the garden, looking bored.
Nata crawled out from under the toad. "Ugh," she said.
"Is it over?" asked the spider.

The deer mouse brushed at the
wet leaves and grasses that clung to Nata.
"Such a mess," she said.
"It could have been worse," said the toad.
The spider slid to the ground and ran to Nata.
"Why didn't you fly?" she cried.
"Yes, Nata," asked the snake, "why didn't you fly?"
Nata looked at them mournfully. "I can't," she said.
"Can't fly?" gasped the bees.
"It happened this morning," said Nata.
"My wings don't work. And they hurt."

Nata buried her face in the mouse's fur and began to cry.

"Don't cry, Nata," said the mouse, patting her gently.

"Don't cry, Nata," said the baby mice, one after another.

The cricket woke up. "Is Nata crying?" he asked.

The bees hovered around Nata, examining her wings.

"They're dry and swollen," they said.

"It's nothing," said the toad.

"How can you say that?" demanded the mice.

"There's nothing worse than not being able to fly," said the bees.

"Oh, I don't know," said the garter snake.

"Try losing your feelers," said the cricket.

Nata stopped crying and sat up. "I feel funny," she said.

Suddenly her wings split open from one end

to the other. "Oh, what is happening?" she cried.

The dry, broken wings drifted to the ground.

In their place were dark, shapeless things that hung limply

down Nata's back. "How awful," she said, looking at them over her shoulder.

"Don't be silly," said the toad. "They're your new wings."

"They don't look like wings," said Nata. "They're ugly."

"They have to dry," said the toad.

Nata sat on a stone and tried to smooth the wrinkled new wings.
They were damp and heavy at first, but as she shook them out and
spread them in the sun, they began to brighten and flash with colors.
"Like a rainbow!" exclaimed the spider.
"But will they work?" asked the bees.
Nata waved her new wings and fluttered into the air.
The baby mice ran beneath her, jumping up and down.
"Lovely!" cried the spider.
"They're perfect," said Nata. "What a nice surprise!"
"It happens every year," said the toad.
"What happens?" asked the garter snake.
"Nobody ever remembers," complained the toad.
"On the first day of summer Nata always gets new wings."
"I do?" asked Nata. "What fun!"

Nata flitted to the cricket and carefully untied his feelers.
"Next time I'll know what is happening
and I won't be so bad," she promised.
"You won't remember," said the toad. "You never do."
Nata laughed. "Of course I'll remember," she said. She soared above the
flowers and the setting sun glinted on her new wings.
The spider rushed to her web to try a new design before dark.
The cricket crawled under a leaf and began to chirp.
The garter snake yawned and slithered away through the grass.
"Good night, Nata," called the baby mice, tumbling through their doorway.
"Good night, you darlings," Nata called back.

Little lights twinkled in the grass as the lightning bugs woke up.

"Nata has new wings," they sang out, launching themselves into the air.

"They're beautiful!"

Nata fluttered among the flowers, deciding where to sleep.

"Thank you," she said politely, snuggling into a rose,

"but I've always had wings."

The toad nodded knowingly. "She's forgotten already," she said.

"Forgotten what?" asked the cricket from under his leaf.

The toad sighed. "Never mind," she said.

She settled herself comfortably in the cool, damp flower bed.

"Anyway," she said, "Nata will be good tomorrow."

"Well, of course," said the cricket. "She always is."

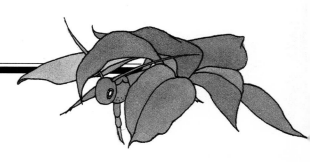

·22·